TOO MUCH TRICK OR TREAT

WRITTEN AND ILLUSTRATED BY

JAYNA MILLER

LANDMARK EDITIONS, INC.

P.O. Box 4469 • 1402 Kansas Avenue • Kansas City, Missouri 64127
(816) 241-4919

Dedicated to
my family —
Dad, Mom,
Julie, Jill,
Grandpa and Grandma.

And to
Aunt Kay Miller and Bob Mercer
for all their help and encouragement.

Second Printing

COPYRIGHT © 1991 BY JAYNA MILLER

International Standard Book Number: 0-933849-37-0 (LIB.BDG.)

Library of Congress Cataloging-in-Publication Data
Miller, Jayna, 1969-
    Too much trick or treat / written and illustrated by Jayna Miller.
    p.   cm.
    Summary: Jammer the Rabbit's classmates get even when Jammer absconds with
all the Halloween treats.
    ISBN 0-933849-37-0 (lib. bdg.)
    [1. Halloween — Fiction.   2. Behavior — Fiction.
    3. Rabbits — Fiction.   4. Animals — Fiction.]

    I. Title.
    PZ7.M6175To   1991
    [Fic] — dc20
                                                    91-14930
                                                    CIP
                                                    AC

Editorial Coordinator: Nancy R. Thatch
Creative Coordinator: David Melton

Printed in the United States of America

Landmark Editions, Inc.
P.O. Box 4469
1402 Kansas Avenue
Kansas City, Missouri 64127
(816) 241-4919

TOO MUCH TRICK OR TREAT

WINNER

GOLD
AWARD

1990

What a wonderful book! It has everything a good Halloween story should have — tricks and treats, an exciting adventure, interesting characters, costumes galore, a deserted house, a strange old woman, a scary night, and enough surprises to delight readers of all ages.

While the text is composed with charm and wit, Jayna's illustrations provide bountiful feasts for the reader's eyes to savor and enjoy. The colors illuminate the scenes in a soft glow, evoking playful reminiscences of the childhood excitement of dressing in costumes and trying to scare the wits out of each other. And there's not a kid alive, or a grownup for that matter, who doesn't enjoy seeing a prankster getting caught in a prank.

When a book is properly designed and illustrated, it projects the illusion that all of the elements of the illustrations were thrown into the air and just happened to fall in the right places. Jayna's illustrations have that look. But she and I know they didn't *just happen*.

To create that illusion of ease, Jayna drew many of her illustrations more than a dozen times. She developed stacks of preliminary drawings of the backgrounds and settings. She drew the characters so many times, she could have drawn them in her sleep. The Halloween costumes for each character had to be designed so the viewer could tell which character was underneath each of the costumes. And the old woman's appearance had to be . . . well . . . you'll see it is not quite what it seems to be.

And that's exactly the way it should be on Halloween.
GOTCHA!

— David Melton
Creative Coordinator
Landmark Editions, Inc.

HALLOWEEN I

"This is going to be the best Halloween ever!" exclaimed Jammer the Rabbit as he put on the meanest, scariest mask he had ever seen. "Gotcha!" he said to himself in the mirror. And then he snickered the way he always did when he was up to no good, which was most of the time.

With a gunnysack slung over his shoulder, Jammer hurried outside and hopped along the path into the woods. He didn't stop to trick-or-treat at any

of the houses. This Halloween he had concocted a scheme for getting more than his usual share of treats.

"Before this night is over," Jammer chuckled, "my sack will be filled with apples, and carrots, and popcorn balls, and ALL THE CHOCOLATE I can eat!"

Just the thought of chocolate made Jammer's nose twitch and his ears flop back and forth. Of all the treats in the world, Jammer liked chocolate best. He didn't care what kind of chocolate he got — sweet, bittersweet, dark brown, or light brown. But chocolate with almonds was his favorite of favorites.

7

Before long Jammer came to the old oak tree at the bend in the path. He couldn't help but snicker as he hid behind the tree to wait. And he didn't have to wait very long. Soon he heard someone walking up the path.

Jammer peeked out from behind the tree and saw a trick-or-treater dressed in a hobo costume. He knew it was Measle the Weasel. Measle's head always

wobbled from side to side as he walked.

When Measle came near the tree, Jammer jumped out and yelled in his most ferocious voice, "Gotcha!"

Measle screamed with fright. He dropped his bag of treats and ran down the path as fast as his legs could carry him.

Jammer roared with laughter. He picked up the bag and poured all of Measle's treats into his own sack. How he enjoyed hearing the chocolate bars drop among the apples and carrots. And he could smell the wonderful creamy kind with almonds. He was just about to take out a bar to munch, when he heard others coming up the path. It had to be Daisy and Clara Raccoon. He would have recognized their giggles anywhere.

When Daisy and Clara came near, Jammer leaped out and yelled, "Gotcha!" That sent the two girls screaming down the path.

"What luck!" Jammer exclaimed as he picked up the bags the raccoons had left behind. Their bags were even fuller than Measle's had been! And Jammer whistled a merry tune as he put the treats into his own sack.

When he heard someone else approaching, Jammer quickly returned to his hiding place. He soon realized it was Bucky the Beaver. Bucky's teeth always made a funny clicking sound.

When Bucky was near enough, Jammer sprang into action. "Gotcha!" he shouted.

Bucky's mouth opened wide with fright and he yelled, "Yipes!" He dropped his bag of treats and ran down the path with his teeth click-clacking all the way.

Jammer whooped and hollered at the fun of it all. He poured Bucky's treats into his own sack, which was now bulging with goodies! Then, not being able to wait another minute, Jammer grabbed a handful of chocolate bars and tore open their wrappers. He sat down and leaned back against the tree.

"They'll never know how I tricked them," he chuckled as he gobbled up the chocolate.

But someone did know. Flatnose the Earthworm, dressed in a pencil costume, was sitting only a few feet away. He had seen the whole thing.

The next morning, when Flatnose told Measle and the others what had happened, they were really angry. They vowed to get even with Jammer the very next Halloween. And they huddled together and made up a plan for doing just that.

"Oh, this is really going to be fun!" Flatnose exclaimed.

15

HALLOWEEN II

The next Halloween Jammer was filled with excitement. His new mask looked even more terrifying than the one he had the year before. And he couldn't wait to scare the others and get another big supply of CHOCOLATE!

Flatnose the Earthworm had a new costume too. This year he knew he would need to move faster. So he wore a train outfit that had two boxcars, a green caboose, and a three-speed engine.

When Jammer came out of his house that night, Flatnose nudged the engine's lever into second gear. Then he quietly followed the rabbit down the path and into the woods.

Jammer didn't plan to hide behind the oak tree again. This time he would surprise everyone by the big willow tree at the far side of the woods.

As soon as Jammer reached the willow tree and stepped behind it, Flatnose turned around. Putting the engine into high gear, he sped lickety-split to where Measle and the others were waiting.

"Jammer is hiding at the big willow tree," the earthworm told them.

"Good work, Flatnose!" Bucky said, clicking his teeth.

"Let's go!" shouted Measle.

And the raccoon girls, of course, giggled with delight as they ran across the bridge with the others.

17

Jammer was becoming impatient. He had waited by the willow tree for a long time. And he was beginning to wonder why no trick-or-treaters had come that way. Then he heard the giggles of Daisy and Clara. When he peeked through the branches, he saw Measle and Bucky were with them. And following at their heels was Flatnose in his train costume.

"Great!" thought Jammer. "I'll get all of their treats at one time!" Then he straightened his mask and prepared to scare them out of their wits.

"I've never *seen* so many chocolate bars!" he heard Daisy giggle.

"With almonds!" exclaimed Bucky, clicking his teeth.

"And she's got lots more chocolate too!" Measle said.

Chocolate? With almonds? And someone has lots more?

Jammer became so excited, he removed his mask and stepped from behind the tree.

"Hi, kids," he said, pretending to be friendly.

"Oh, hi, Jammer," said Measle, holding up a fistful of bars. "Have you ever seen so much chocolate?"

"And there's more too," said Clara.

"There are mountains of chocolate!" giggled Daisy.

"With almonds!" clicked Bucky.

"Where?" Jammer had to know.

"At the old Wilson house," Clara replied.

"But no one lives at the Wilson house anymore," Jammer said.

"A woman moved in last week," Daisy told him.

"And she's really nice," said Measle. "She's decorated the whole house just for Halloween."

20

"The house looks awfully spooky," said Clara. "And upstairs she has *pounds* and *pounds* of chocolate!"

"With almonds!" clicked Bucky.

"She told us to take all we wanted!" added Measle.

"Wow!" Jammer exclaimed. "I'm going to need a bigger sack!" And without even saying "good-bye," he jumped over the fence and scurried home to get one.

The dust hadn't settled from his tracks before Measle and the others turned around and ran back down the path as fast as they could. Flatnose's engine sped along in top gear.

Wasting no time at home, Jammer grabbed the biggest sack he could find. Then he headed toward the old Wilson house, whistling every step of the way…until…

He reached the rusted gate in front of the house. As the clouds drifted apart and let the light of the moon shine on the house, Jammer stopped in his tracks.

Clara had been right. The house did look spooky. It was old and gray, and ready to fall to the ground. Jammer couldn't help but wonder why a nice old woman would want to live in such an awful place.

When the clouds covered the moon again, the night seemed even darker than before. A shiver ran up and down Jammer's spine. He wasn't sure he

wanted to go into that house alone. He wished Measle and the others were with him.

But then Jammer thought of the chocolate.

"Mountains of it!" Daisy had said.

"With almonds!" Bucky had clicked.

"Take all you want!" Measle had added.

It was too much for a *chocoholic* like Jammer to resist. So he took a deep breath and started toward the house. When he reached the front porch, he stepped up. Then, with all the courage he could find, he raised his hand and knocked on the door. There was no answer. So he knocked again. When the door slowly opened before him, its rusted hinges moaned and groaned.

Jammer peered into the darkness and saw an old woman standing by the staircase. She was wearing a long white dress. And her white hair, piled high on her head, looked like matted spider webs twisted into a knot. Her face was all withered and wrinkled like a dried prune.

"Trick or treat," Jammer finally said, trying not to sound frightened.

"Oh, *treat* of course," the woman replied in a scratchy voice. "Did you come to get some of my chocolate?"

"Yes, Ma'am," Jammer said with nervous politeness.

"Come right in," the woman told him. "The chocolate is in the room at the top of the stairs. Go right up."

"And may I take all the chocolate I want?" he asked.

"With almonds," the woman said with a smile.

As Jammer climbed the stairs, the steps creaked beneath his feet. When he got to the top, he walked to the doorway and looked into the room. By flickering candlelight, he could see that Measle and the others had told the truth—there were mountains of chocolate bars heaped and stacked on the tabletop!

"What a terrific sight!" Jammer exclaimed. Forgetting his fear, he ran to the table and started grabbing up chocolate bars and dropping them into his sack.

"Take all you want," he heard the old woman say.

When he turned around, he saw she was standing in the doorway. He hadn't realized the woman had followed him up the stairs.

"Maybe I should leave some for the other trick-or-treaters," Jammer said, starting to feel uneasy.

"Nonsense," the woman replied. "There won't be any more trick-or-treaters coming by this late at night."

Jammer had forgotten all about the time. He suddenly realized how late it was. And he began to wonder how he could get past the old woman and out the door.

"I think I have plenty of chocolate," he said.

"You never have *plenty* until you have *too much*," the woman told him. "And you do like chocolate, don't you?" she asked, clicking her teeth.

"Yes, Ma'am," Jammer replied.

"I like chocolate too," the woman said with a crooked smile spreading across her wrinkled face. "But there is one thing I like even more than chocolate. Do you want to know what that is?"

"What?" asked Jammer, not sure he really wanted to hear the answer.

The old woman reached out her hands and yelled, "RABBIT STEW!"

Jammer dropped his sack of treats and scurried under the table before the woman could grab him.

Suddenly all the shutters on the windows started banging open and shut. The closet door fell from its hinges. A skeleton stepped out of the shadows. A ghost swung down from the ceiling. And the screeching sound of a train whistle pierced the air.

Jammer screamed with fright and jumped to his feet. He ran to the window and leaped out. Then he tumbled head over heels across the porch roof and dropped to the ground.

As he raced toward the gate, he heard laughter coming from the house. But he didn't turn around to see who was laughing. He pushed open the gate and ran for home.

For some time the old woman stood at the front door and laughed and laughed. Then her form began to change shape as Bucky climbed down from Measle's shoulders and took off the wrinkled mask. Daisy was still giggling as she let her ghost sheet drop to the floor. And Clara giggled even more as she stepped out of her skeleton costume. Declaring total victory, Flatnose tooted his whistle three times.

28

The next day at school, Jammer the Rabbit was very quiet.

"What's the matter?" Bucky asked him with a click.

"Oh, nothing," Jammer replied. "I guess I just had too much trick or treat."

"Nonsense," said Flatnose. "There's no such thing as *too much* trick or treat."

Then Bucky stepped up to Jammer. "Do you know what I like better than chocolate?" he said. "RABBIT STEW!"

And everyone howled with laughter, except Jammer the Rabbit. He didn't think it was funny at all.

THE NATIONAL WRITTEN & ILLUSTRATED

— THE 1989 NATIONAL AWARD WINNING BOOKS —

Lauren Peters
age 7

Michael Cain
age 11

Problems at the North Pole
Written & illustrated by Lauren Peters

the Legend of SIR MIGUEL
MICHAEL CAIN

WE ARE A THUNDERSTORM
written and photographed by amity gaige

—THE 1987 NATIONAL AWARD WINNING BOOKS—

Amity Gaige
age 16

JOSHUA DISOBEYS
Written and Illustrated by Dennis Vollmer

THE HALF & HALF DOG
written and illustrated by LISA GROSS

who owns The sun?
~written & illustrated by~ STACY CHBOSKY

—THE 1989 GOLD AWARD WINNERS—

Dennis Vollmer
age 6

BROKEN ARROW BOY
WRITTEN AND ILLUSTRATED BY ADAM MOORE and his friends

GET THAT GOAT!
WRITTEN AND ILLUSTRATED BY MICHAEL AUSHENKER

Lisa Gross
age 12

Students' Winning Books Motivate and Inspire

Each year it is Landmark's pleasure to publish the winning books of The National Written & Illustrated By... Awards Contest For Students. These are important books because they supply such positive motivation and inspiration for other talented students to write and illustrate books too!

Students of All Ages Love the Winning Books

Students of all ages enjoy reading these fascinating books created by our young author/illustrators. When students see the beautiful books, printed in full color and handsomely bound in hardback covers, they, too, will become excited about writing and illustrating books and eager to enter them in the Contest.

Enter Your Book In the Next Contest

If you are 6 to 19 years of age you may enter the Contest too. Perhaps your book may be one of the next winners and you will become a published author and illustrator too.

Stacy Chbosky
age 14

Adam Moore
age 9

Michael Aushenker
age 19

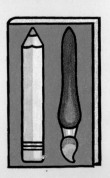

BY... AWARDS CONTEST FOR STUDENTS
— THE 1988 NATIONAL AWARD WINNING BOOKS —

Leslie Ann MacKeen
age 9

—THE 1986 NATIONAL AWARD WINNING BOOKS—

Elizabeth Haidle
age 13

Heidi Salter
age 19

— THE 1985 GOLD AWARD WINNERS —

Winners Receive Contracts, Royalties and Scholarships

The National Written & Illustrated by... Contest Is an Annual Event! There is no entry fee! The winners receive publishing contracts, royalties on the sale of their books, and all-expense-paid trips to our offices in Kansas City, Missouri, where professional editors and art directors assist them in preparing their final manuscripts and illustrations for publication.

Winning Students Receive Scholarships Too! The R.D. and Joan Dale Hubbard Foundation will award a total of $30,000 in scholarship certificates to the winners and the four runners-up in all three age categories. Each winner receives a $5,000 scholarship; those in Second Place are awarded a $2,000 scholarship; and those in Third, Fourth, and Fifth Places receive a $1,000 scholarship.

To obtain Contest Rules, send a self-addressed, stamped, business-size envelope to: THE NATIONAL WRITTEN & ILLUSTRATED BY... AWARDS CONTEST FOR STUDENTS, Landmark Editions, Inc., P.O. Box 4469, Kansas City, MO 64127.

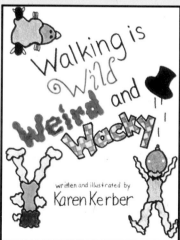

Amy Hagstrom
age 9

Isaac Whitlatch
age 11

Karen Kerber
age 12

David McAdoo
age 14

Dav Pilkey
age 19

THE WRITTEN & ILLUSTRATED BY... CONTEST

— THE 1990 NATIONAL AWARD WINNING BOOKS —

Aruna Chandrasekhar
age 9

Anika Thomas
age 13

Cara Reichel
age 15

Jonathan Kahn
age 9

Jayna Miller
age 19

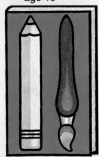

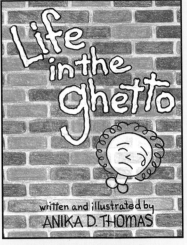

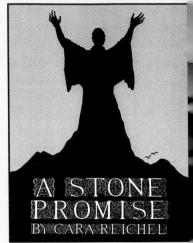

— THE 1990 GOLD AWARD WINNERS —

Winning the Gold Award and having my book published are two of the most exciting things that have ever happened to me! If you are a student between 6 and 19 years of age, and you like to write and draw, then create a book of your own and enter it in the Contest. Who knows? Maybe your book will be one of the next winners, and you will become a published author and illustrator too.

— Jayna Miller
Author and Illustrator
TOO MUCH TRICK OR TREAT

E   Miller, Jayna
Mil
                                7535
            Too much trick or
            treat